This book belongs to:

....

....

Paddy pretended to be terribly frightened. *Page 80.*

A BEDTIME STORY-BOOK

THE

ADVENTURES OF

Paddy
BEAVER

THORNTON W. BURGESS

LITTLE, BROWN AND COMPANY

BOSTON   TORONTO

Republished in 1987

Library of Congress Cataloging-in-Publication Data

Burgess, Thornton W. (Thornton Waldo), 1874-1965.
The adventures of Paddy Beaver.

(A Bedtime story-book)
Summary: Chronicles the adventures of Paddy Beaver
and his animal friends in Green Meadow.

[1. Beavers–Fiction. 2. Animals–Fiction]
I. Title.   II. Series.
PZ7.B917Add   1987   [E]   87-3035
ISBN 0-316-11628-9 (pbk.)

Illustrations by Harrison Cady

PRINTED AND BOUND IN CANADA

CONTENTS

THE ADVENTURES OF PADDY THE BEAVER

I

PADDY THE BEAVER BEGINS WORK

> Work, work all the night
> While the stars are shining bright;
> Work, work all the day;
> I have got no time to play.

THIS little rhyme Paddy the Beaver made up as he toiled at building the dam which was to make the pond he so much desired deep in the Green Forest. Of course it wasn't quite true, that about working all night and all day. Nobody could do that, you know, and keep it up. Everybody has to rest and sleep. Yes, and everybody has to play a little to be

at their best. So it wasn't quite true
that Paddy worked all day after working all night. But it was true that
Paddy had no time to play. He had
too much to do. He had had his playtime during the long summer, and now
he had to get ready for the long cold
winter.

Now of all the little workers in the
Green Forest, on the Green Meadows,
and in the Smiling Pool, none can com-
pare with Paddy the Beaver, not even
his cousin, Jerry Muskrat. Happy
Jack Squirrel and Striped Chipmunk
store up food for the long cold months
when rough Brother North Wind and
Jack Frost rule, and Jerry Muskrat
builds a fine house wherein to keep
warm and comfortable, but all this is
as nothing to the work of Paddy the
Beaver.

As I said before, Paddy had had a

long playtime through the summer.
He had wandered up and down the
Laughing Brook. He had followed it
way up to the place where it started.
And all the time he had been studying
and studying to make sure that he
wanted to stay in the Green Forest.
In the first place, he had to be sure that
there was plenty of the kind of food
that he likes.   Then he had to be equal-
ly sure that he could make a pond near
where this particular food grew. Last
of all, he had to satisfy himself that if
he did make a pond and build a home,
he would be reasonably safe in it.
And all these things he had done in his
playtime. Now he was ready to go to
work, and when Paddy begins work, he
sticks to it until it is finished. He says
that is the only way to succeed, and you
know and I know that he is right.

Now Paddy the Beaver can see at

night just as Reddy Fox and Peter
Rabbit and Bobby Coon can, and he
likes the night best, because he feels
safest then.   But he can see in the daytime too, and when he feels that he is
perfectly safe and no one is watching,
he works then too.   Of course the first
thing to do was to build a dam across
the Laughing Brook to make the pond
he so much needed.   He chose a low
open place deep in the Green Forest,
around the edge of which grew many
young aspen-trees, the bark of which
is his favorite food.   Through the middle of this open place flowed the Laughing Brook.   At the lower edge was just
the place for a dam.   It would not have
to be very long, and when it was finished and the water was stopped in the
Laughing Brook, it would just have to
flow over the low open place and make
a pond there.   Paddy's eyes twinkled

when he first saw it.   It was right then
that he made up his mind to stay in the
Green Forest.

So now that he was ready to begin
his dam he went up the Laughing Brook
to a place where alders and willows
grew, and there he began work; that
work was the cutting of a great number
of trees by means of his big front teeth
which were given him for just this pur-
pose.   And as he worked, Paddy was
happy, for one can never be truly
happy who does no work.

II

PADDY PLANS A POND

PADDY THE BEAVER was busy cutting down trees for the dam he had planned to build. Up in the woods of the North from which he had come to the Green Forest he had learned all about tree-cutting and dam-building and canal-digging and house-building. Paddy's father and mother had been very wise in the ways of the Beaver world, and Paddy had been quick to learn. So now he knew just what to do and the best way of doing it. You know a great many people waste time and labor doing things the wrong way, so that they have to be done over again. They forget to be sure they are right, and so they go ahead until they find they are wrong, and all their work goes for nothing.

But Paddy the Beaver isn't this kind. Paddy would never have leaped into the spring with the steep sides without looking, as Grandfather Frog did. So now he carefully picked out the trees to cut. He could not afford to waste time cutting down a tree that wasn't going to be just what he wanted when it was down. When he was sure that the tree was right, he looked up at the top to find out whether, when he had cut it, it would fall clear of other trees. He had learned to do that when he was quite young and heedless. He remembered just how he had felt when after working hard, oh, so hard, to cut a big tree, he had warned all his friends to get out of the way so that they would not be hurt when it fell, and then it hadn't fallen at all because the top had caught in another tree. He was so mortified that he didn't get over it for a long time.

So now he made sure that a tree was going to fall clear and just where he wanted it. Then he sat up on his hind legs, and with his great broad tail for a brace, began to make the chips fly. You know Paddy has the most wonderful teeth for cutting. They are long and broad and sharp. He would begin by making a deep bite, and then another just a little way below. Then he would pry out the little piece of wood between. When he had cut very deep on one side so that the tree would fall that way, he would work around to the other side. Just as soon as the tree began to lean and he was sure that it was going to fall, he would scamper away so as to be out of danger. He loved to see those tall trees lean forward slowly, then faster and faster, till they struck the ground with a crash.

Just as soon as they were down, he would trim off the branches until the trees were just long poles. This was easy work, for he could take off a good-sized branch with one bite. On many he left their bushy tops. When he had trimmed them to suit him and had cut them into the right lengths, he would tug and pull them down to the place where he meant to build his dam.

There he placed the poles side by side, not across the Laughing Brook like a bridge, but with the big ends pointing up the Laughing Brook, which was quite broad but shallow right there. To keep them from floating away, he rolled stones and piled mud on the bushy ends. Clear across on both sides he laid those poles until the land began

to rise. Then he dragged more poles
and piled on top of these and wedged
short sticks crosswise between them.

And all the time the Laughing Brook
was having harder and harder work to
run. Its merry laugh grew less merry
and finally almost stopped, because, you
see, the water could not get through between all those poles and sticks fast
enough. It was just about that time
that the little people of the Smiling
Pool decided that it was time to see
just what Paddy was doing, and they
started up the Laughing Brook, leaving
only Grandfather Frog and the tad-
poles in the Smiling Pool, which for a
little while would smile no more.

III

PADDY HAS MANY VISITORS

PADDY THE BEAVER knew perfectly well that he would have visitors just as soon as he began to build his dam. He expected a lot of them. You see, he knew that none of them ever had seen a Beaver at work unless perhaps it was Prickly Porky the Porcupine, who also had come down from the North. So as he worked he kept his ears open, and he smiled to himself as he heard a little rustle here and then a little rustle there. He knew just what those little rustles meant. Each one meant another visitor. Yes, Sir, each rustle meant another visitor, and yet not one had shown himself.

Paddy chuckled. "Seems to me

that you are dreadfully afraid to show
yourselves," said he in a loud voice,
just as if he were talking to nobody in
particular.   Everything   was   still.
There wasn't so much as a rustle after
Paddy   spoke.   He   chuckled   again.
He could just *feel* ever so many eyes
watching him, though he didn't see a
single pair. And he knew that the
reason his visitors were hiding so carefully was because they were afraid of
him. You see, Paddy was much bigger
than most of the little meadow and
forest people, and they didn't know
what kind of a temper he might have.
It is always safest to be very distrustful
of strangers. That is one of the very
first things taught all little meadow and
forest children.

Of course, Paddy knew all about this.
He had been brought up that way.
"Be sure, and then you'll never be

sorry" had been one of his mother's favorite sayings, and he had always remembered it. Indeed, it had saved him
a great deal of trouble. So now he was
perfectly willing to go right on working
and let his hidden visitors watch him
until they were sure that he meant them
no harm. You see, he himself felt
quite sure that none of them was big
enough to do him any harm. Little Joe
Otter was the only one he had any
doubts about, and he felt quite sure that
Little Joe wouldn't try to pick a quar-
rel. So he kept right on cutting trees,
trimming off the branches, and hauling
the trunks down to the dam he was
building. Some of them he floated
down the Laughing Brook. This was
easier.

Now when the little people of the
Smiling Pool, who were the first to find
out that Paddy the Beaver had come to

the Green Forest, had started up the
Laughing Brook to see what he was doing, they had told the Merry Little
Breezes where they were going. The
Merry Little Breezes had been greatly
excited. They couldn't understand
how a stranger could have been living
in the Green Forest without their
knowledge. You see, they quite forgot
that they very seldom wandered to the
deepest part of the Green Forest. Of
course they started at once as fast as
they could go to tell all the other little
people who live on or around the Green
Meadows, all but Old Man Coyote.
For some reason they thought it best
not to tell him. They were a little
doubtful about Old Man Coyote. He
was so big and strong and so sly and
smart that all his neighbors were
afraid of him. Perhaps the Merry
Little Breezes had this fact in mind,

and knew that none would dare go to call on the stranger if they knew that Old Man Coyote was going too. Anyway, they simply passed the time of day with Old Man Coyote and hurried on to tell every one else, and the very last one they met was Sammy Jay.

Sammy was terribly put out to think that anything should be going on that he didn't know about first. You know he is very fond of prying into the affairs of other people, and he loves dearly to boast that there is nothing going on in the Green Forest or on the Green Meadows that he doesn't know about. So now his pride was hurt, and he was in a terrible rage as he started after the Merry Little Breezes for the place deep in the Green Forest where they said Paddy the Beaver was at work. He didn't believe a word of it, but he would see for himself.

IV

SAMMY JAY SPEAKS HIS MIND

WHEN Sammy Jay reached the place deep in the Green Forest where Paddy the Beaver was so hard at work, he didn't hide as had the little four-footed people. You see, of course, he had no reason to hide, because he felt perfectly safe. Paddy had just cut a big tree, and it fell with a crash as Sammy came hurrying up. Sammy was so surprised that for a minute he couldn't find his tongue. He had not supposed that anybody but Farmer Brown or Farmer Brown's boy could cut down so large a tree as that, and it quite took his breath away. But he got it again in a minute. He was boiling with anger, anyway, to think that he should have been the last to learn that Paddy had come down from the North to make his home in the Green Forest, and here was a chance to speak his mind.

"Thief! thief! thief!" he screamed in his harshest voice.

Paddy the Beaver looked up with a twinkle in his eyes. "Hello, Mr. Jay! I see you haven't any better manners than your cousin who lives up where I came from," said he.

"Thief! thief! thief!" screamed Sammy, hopping up and down, he was so angry.

"Meaning yourself, I suppose," said Paddy. "I never did see an honest Jay, and I don't suppose I ever will."

"Ha, ha, ha!" laughed Peter Rabbit, who had quite forgotten that he was hiding.

"Oh, how do you do, Mr. Rabbit? I'm very glad you have called on me this morning," said Paddy, just as if he hadn't known all the time just where Peter was. "Mr. Jay seems to have gotten out of the wrong side of his bed this morning."

Peter laughed again. "He always does," said he. "If he didn't, he wouldn't be happy. You wouldn't think it to look at him, but he is happy right now. He doesn't know it, but he is. He always is happy when he can show what a bad temper he has."

Sammy Jay glared down at Peter. Then he glared at Paddy. And all the time he still shrieked "Thief!" as hard as ever he could. Paddy kept right on working, paying no attention to Sammy. This made Sammy more angry than ever. He kept coming nearer and nearer until at last he was in the very tree that Paddy happened to be cutting. Paddy's eyes twinkled.

"I'm no thief!" he exclaimed suddenly.

"You are! You are! Thief! Thief!" shrieked Sammy. "You're stealing our trees!"

"They're not your trees," retorted Paddy. "They belong to the Green Forest, and the Green Forest belongs to all who love it, and we all have a perfect right to take what we need from it. I need these trees, and I've just as much right to take them as you have to take the fat acorns that drop in the fall.

"No such thing!" screamed Sammy. You know he can't talk without screaming, and the more excited he gets, the louder he screams. "No such thing! Acorns are food. They are meant to eat. I have to have them to live. But you are cutting down whole trees.

You are spoiling the Green Forest. You don't belong here. Nobody invited you, and nobody wants you. You're a thief!"

Then up spoke Jerry Muskrat, who, you know, is cousin to Paddy the Beaver.

"Don't you mind him," said he, pointing at Sammy Jay. "Nobody does. He's the greatest trouble-maker in the Green Forest or on the Green Meadows. He would steal from his own relatives. Don't mind what he says, Cousin Paddy."

Now all this time Paddy had been working away just as if no one was around. Just as Jerry stopped speaking, Paddy thumped the ground with his tail, which is his way of warning people to watch out, and suddenly scurried away as fast as he could run. Sammy Jay was so surprised that he

couldn't find his tongue for a minute,
and he didn't notice anything peculiar
about that tree. Then suddenly he felt
himself falling. With a frightened
scream, he spread his wings to fly, but
branches of the tree swept him down
with them right into the Laughing
Brook.

You see while Sammy had been
speaking his mind, Paddy the Beaver
had cut down the very tree in which he
was sitting.

Sammy wasn't hurt, but he was wet
and muddy and terribly frightened,—
the most miserable looking Jay that
ever was seen. It was too much for all
the little people who were hiding.
They just had to laugh. Then they all
came out to pay their respects to Paddy
the Beaver.

V

PADDY KEEPS HIS PROMISE

PADDY THE BEAVER kept right on working just as if he hadn't any visitors. You see, it is a big undertaking to build a dam. And when that was done there was a house to build and a supply of food for the winter to cut and store. Oh, Paddy the Beaver had no time for idle gossip, you may be sure! So he kept right on building his dam. It didn't look much like a dam at first, and some of Paddy's visitors turned up their noses when they first saw it. They had heard stories of what a wonderful dam-builder Paddy was, and they had expected to see something like the smooth, grass-covered bank with which Farmer

Brown kept the Big River from running back on his low lands. Instead, all they saw was a great pile of poles and sticks which looked like anything but a dam.

"Pooh!" exclaimed Billy Mink, "I guess we needn't worry about the Laughing Brook and the Smiling Pool, if that is the best Paddy can do. Why, the water of the Laughing Brook will work through that in no time."

Of course Paddy heard him, but he said nothing, just kept right on working.

"Just look at the way he has laid those sticks!" continued Billy Mink. "Seems as if any one would know enough to lay them *across* the Laughing Brook instead of just the other way. I could build a better dam than that."

Paddy said nothing; he just kept right on working.

"Yes, Sir," Billy boasted. "I could build a better dam than that. Why, that pile of sticks will never stop the water."

"Is something the matter with your eyesight, Billy Mink?" inquired Jerry Muskrat.

"Of course not!" retorted Billy indignantly. "Why?"

"Oh, nothing much, only you don't seem to notice that already the Laughing Brook is over its banks above Paddy's dam," replied Jerry, who had been studying the dam with a great deal of interest.

Billy looked a wee bit foolish, for sure enough there was a little pool just above the dam, and it was growing bigger.

Paddy still kept at work, saying nothing. He was digging in front of the dam now, and the mud and grass he

dug up he stuffed in between the ends
of the sticks and patted down with his
hands. He did this all along the front
of the dam and on top of it too, wherever he thought it was needed. Of
course this made it harder for the water
to work through, and the little pond
above the dam began to grow faster.
It wasn't a great while before it was
nearly to the top of the dam, which at
first was very low. Then Paddy
brought more sticks. This was easier
now, because he could float them down
from where he was cutting. He would
put them in place on the top of the dam,
then hurry for more. Wherever it was
needed, he would put in mud. He even
rolled a few stones in to help hold the
mass.

So the dam grew and grew, and so did
the pond above the dam. Of course, it
took a good many days to build so big a

dam, and a lot of hard work! Every
morning the little people of the Green
Forest and the Green Meadows would
visit it, and every morning they would
find that it had grown a great deal in
the night, for that is when Paddy likes
best to work.

By this time, the Laughing Brook
had stopped laughing, and down in the
Smiling Pool there was hardly water
enough for the minnows to feel safe a
minute. Billy Mink had stopped making fun of the dam, and all the little
people who live in the Laughing Brook
and the Smiling Pool were terribly
worried.

To be sure Paddy had warned them
of what he was going to do, and had
promised that just as soon as his pond
was big enough, the water would once
more run in the Laughing Brook.
They tried to believe him, but they

couldn't help having just a wee bit of
fear that he might not be wholly honest.
You see, they didn't know him, for he
was a stranger. Jerry Muskrat was
the only one who seemed absolutely sure
that everything would be all right.
Perhaps that was because Paddy is his
cousin, and Jerry couldn't help but feel
proud of such a big cousin and one who
was so smart.

So day by day the dam grew, and the
pond grew, and then one morning
Grandfather Frog, down in what had
once been the Smiling Pool, heard a
sound that made his heart jump for joy.
It was a murmur that kept growing and
growing, until at last it was the merry
laugh of the Laughing Brook. Then
he knew that Paddy had kept his word
and water would once more fill the
Smiling Pool.

VI

NOW it happened that the very
day before Paddy the Beaver
decided that his pond was big
enough, and so allowed the water to run
in the Laughing Brook once more,
Farmer Brown's boy took it into his
head to go fishing in the Smiling Pool.
Just as usual he went whistling down
across the Green Meadows. Somehow,
when he goes fishing, he always feels
like whistling. Grandfather Frog
heard him coming and dived into the
little bit of water remaining in the
Smiling Pool and stirred up the mud
at the bottom so that Farmer Brown's
boy shouldn't see him.

Nearer and nearer drew the whistle.
Suddenly it stopped right short off.
Farmer Brown's boy had come in sight
of the Smiling Pool or rather, it was
what used to be the Smiling Pool.
Now there wasn't any Smiling Pool,
for the very little pool left was too
small and sickly-looking to smile.
There were great banks of mud, out of
which grew the bulrushes. The lily-
pads were forlornly stretched out towards the tiny pool of water remaining.
Where the banks were steep and high,
the holes that Jerry Muskrat and Billy
Mink knew so well were plain to see.
Over at one side stood Jerry Muskrat's
house, wholly out of water.

Somehow, it seemed to Farmer
Brown's boy that he must be dreaming.
He never, never had seen anything like
this before, not even in the very driest
weather of the hottest part of the sum-

mer. He looked this way and looked that way. The Green Meadows looked just as usual. The Green Forest looked just as usual. The Laughing Brook—ha! What was the matter with the Laughing Brook? He couldn't hear it and that, you know, was very unusual. He dropped his rod and ran over to the Laughing Brook. There wasn't any brook. No, sir, there wasn't any brook; just pools of water with the tiniest of streams trickling between. Big stones over which he had always seen the water running in the prettiest of little white falls were bare and dry. In the little pools frightened minnows were darting about.

Farmer Brown's boy scratched his head in a puzzled way. "I don't understand it," said he. "I don't understand it at all. Something must have

gone wrong with the springs that supply the water for the Laughing Brook.
They must have failed. Yes, Sir, that
is just what must have happened. But
I never heard of such a thing happen-
ing before, and I really don't see how it
could happen." He stared up into the
Green Forest just as if he thought he
could see those springs. Of course, he
didn't think anything of the kind. He
was just turning it all over in his mind.
"I know what I'll do! I'll go up to
those springs this afternoon and find
out what the trouble is," he said out
loud. "They are way over almost on
the other side of the Green Forest, and
the easiest way to get there will be to
start from home and cut across the Old
Pasture up to the edge of the Mountain
behind the Green Forest. If I try to
follow up the Laughing Brook now, it
will take too long, because it winds and

twists so. Besides, it is too hard
work.''

With that, Farmer Brown's boy went
back and picked up his rod. Then he
started for home across the Green
Meadows, and for once he wasn't whistling. You see, he was too busy thinking. In fact, he was so busy thinking
that he didn't see Jimmy Skunk until
he almost stepped on him, and then he
gave a frightened jump and ran, for
without a gun he was just as much
afraid of Jimmy as Jimmy was of him
when he did have a gun.

Jimmy just grinned and went on
about his business. It always tickles
Jimmy to see people run away from
him, especially people so much bigger
than himself; they look so silly.

''I should think that they would have
learned by this time that if they don't
bother me, I won't bother them,'' he

muttered, as he rolled over a stone to look for fat beetles. "Somehow, folks never seem to understand me."

VII

FARMER BROWN'S BOY GETS ANOTHER SURPRISE

ACROSS the Old Pasture to the foot of the Mountain back of the Green Forest tramped Farmer Brown's boy. Ahead of him trotted Bowser the Hound, sniffing and snuffing for the tracks of Reddy or Granny Fox. Of course he didn't find them, for Reddy and Granny hadn't been up in the Old Pasture for a long time. But he did find old Jed Thumper, the big gray Rabbit who had made things so uncomfortable for Peter Rabbit once upon a time, and gave him such a fright that old Jed didn't look where he was going and almost ran headfirst into Farmer Brown's boy.

"Hi, there, you old cottontail!" yelled Farmer Brown's boy, and this frightened Old Jed still more, so that he actually ran right past his own castle of bullbriars without seeing it.

Farmer Brown's boy kept on his way, laughing at the fright of old Jed Thumper. Presently he reached the springs from which came the water that made the very beginning of the Laughing Brook. He expected to find them dry, for way down on the Green Meadows the Smiling Pool was nearly dry, and the Laughing Brook was nearly dry, and he had supposed that of course the reason was that the springs where the Laughing Brook started were no longer bubbling.

But they were! The clear cold water came bubbling up out of the ground just as it always had, and ran off down into the Green Forest in a little stream that would grow and grow as it ran and become the Laughing Brook. Farmer Brown's boy took off his ragged old straw hat and scowled down at the bubbling water just as if he thought it had no business to be bubbling there.

Of course, he didn't think just that. The fact is, he didn't know just what he did think. Here were the springs bubbling away just as they always had. There was the little stream starting off down into the Green Forest with a gurgle that by and by would become a laugh, just as it always had. And yet down on the Green Meadows on the other side of the Green Forest there was no longer a Laughing Brook or a Smiling Pool. He felt as if he ought to pinch himself to make sure that he was awake and not dreaming.

"I don't know what it means," said he, talking out loud. "No, Sir, I don't know what it means at all, but I'm going to find out. There's a cause for everything in this world, and when a fellow doesn't know a thing, it is his business to find out all about it. I'm going to find out what has happened to the Laughing Brook, if it takes me a year!"

With that he started to follow the little stream which ran gurgling down into the Green Forest. He had followed that little stream more than once, and now he found it just as he remembered it. The farther it ran, the larger it grew, until at last it became the Laughing Brook, merrily tumbling over rocks and making deep pools in which the trout loved to hide. At last he came to the edge of a little open hollow in the very heart of the Green Forest. He knew what splendid deep holes there were in the Laughing Brook here, and how the big trout loved to lie in

them because they were deep and cool.
He was thinking of these trout now
and wishing that he had brought along
his fishing-rod. He pushed his way
through a thicket of alders and then—
Farmer Brown's boy stopped suddenly
and fairly gasped! He had to stop because there right in front of him was a
pond!

He rubbed his eyes and looked again.
Then he stooped down and put his hand
in the water to see if it was real. There
was no doubt about it. It was real water,—a real pond where there never had
been a pond before. It was very still
there in the heart of the Green Forest.
It was always very still there, but it
seemed stiller than usual as he tramped
around the edge of this strange pond.
He felt as if it were all a dream. He
wondered if pretty soon he wouldn't
wake up and find it all untrue. But he

didn't, and so he kept on tramping until presently he came to a dam,—a splendid dam of logs and sticks and mud. Over the top of it the water was running, and down in the Green Forest below he could hear the Laughing Brook just beginning to laugh once more. Farmer Brown's boy sat down with his elbows on his knees and his chin in his hands. He was almost too much surprised to even think.

VIII

PETER RABBIT GETS A DUCKING

FARMER BROWN'S boy sat with his chin in his hands staring at the new pond in the Green Forest and at the dam which had made it. That dam puzzled him. Who could have built it? What did they build it for? Why hadn't he heard them chopping? He looked carelessly at the stump of one of the trees, and then a still more puzzled look made deep furrows between his eyes. It looked— yes, it looked very much as if teeth, and not an axe, had cut down that tree. Farmer Brown's boy stared and stared, his mouth gaping wide open. He looked so funny that Peter Rabbit, who was hiding under an old pile of brush close by, nearly laughed right out.

But Peter didn't laugh. No, Sir, Peter didn't laugh, for just that very minute something happened. Sniff! Sniff! That was right behind him at the very edge of the old brush-pile, and every hair on Peter stood on end with fright.

"Bow, wow, wow!" It seemed to Peter that the great voice was right in his very ears. It frightened him so that he just *had* to jump. He didn't have time to think. And so he jumped right out from under the pile of brush and of course right into plain sight. And the very instant he jumped there came another great roar behind him. Of course it was from Bowser the Hound. You see, Bowser had been following the trail of his master, but as he always stops to sniff at everything he passes, he had been some distance behind. When he came to the pile of brush under which Peter was hiding he had sniffed at that, and of course he had smelled Peter right away.

Now when Peter jumped out so suddenly, he had landed right at one end of the dam. The second roar of Bowser's great voice frightened him still more, and he jumped right up on the dam. There was nothing for him to do now but go across, and it wasn't the best of going. No, indeed, it wasn't the best of going. You see, it was mostly a tangle of sticks. Happy Jack Squirrel or Chatterer the Red Squirrel or Striped Chipmunk would have skipped across it without the least trouble. But Peter Rabbit has no sharp little claws with which to cling to logs and sticks, and right away he was in a peck of trouble. He slipped down between the sticks, scrambled out, slipped again, and then, trying to make a long jump, he lost his balance and—tumbled heels over head into the water!

Poor Peter Rabbit! He gave himself up for lost this time. He could swim, but at best he is a poor swimmer and doesn't like the water. He couldn't dive and keep out of sight like Jerry Muskrat or Billy Mink. All he could do was to paddle as fast as his legs would go. The water had gone up his nose and down his throat so that he choked, and all the time he felt sure that Bowser the Hound would plunge in after him and catch him. And if he shouldn't, why Farmer Brown's Boy would simply wait for him to come ashore and then catch him.

But Farmer Brown's boy didn't do anything of the kind. No, Sir, he didn't.

Instead he shouted to Bowser and called him away. Bowser didn't want to come, but he long ago learned to obey, and very slowly he walked over to where his master was sitting.

"You know it wouldn't be fair, old fellow, to try to catch Peter now. It wouldn't be fair at all, and we never want to do anything unfair, do we?" said he. Perhaps Bowser didn't agree, but he wagged his tail as if he did, and sat down beside his master to watch Peter swim.

It seemed to Peter as if he never, never would reach the shore, though really it was only a very little distance that he had to swim. When he did scramble out, he was a sorry looking Rabbit. He didn't waste any time, but started for home as fast as he could go, lipperty—lipperty—lip. And Farmer Brown's boy and Bowser the Hound just laughed and didn't try to catch him at all.

"Well, I never!" exclaimed Sammy Jay, who had seen it all from the top of a pine-tree. "Well, I never! I guess Farmer Brown's boy isn't so bad, after all."

IX

PADDY PLANS A HOUSE

PADDY THE BEAVER sat on his dam, and his eyes shone with happiness as he looked out over the shining water of the pond he had made. All around the edge of it grew the tall trees of the Green Forest. It was very beautiful and very still and very lonesome. That is, it would have seemed lonesome to almost any one but Paddy the Beaver. But Paddy never is lonesome. You see, he finds company in the trees and flowers and all the little plants.

It was still, very, very still. Over on one side was a beautiful rosy glow in the water. It was the reflection from

jolly, round, red Mr. Sun. Paddy
couldn't see him because of the tall
trees, but he knew exactly what Mr.
Sun was doing. He was going to bed
behind the Purple Hills. Pretty soon
the little stars would come out and
twinkle down at him. He loves the little stars and always watches for the
first one.

Yes, Paddy the Beaver was very
happy. He would have been perfectly
happy but for one thing: Farmer
Brown's boy had found his dam and
pond that very afternoon, and Paddy
wasn't quite sure what Farmer
Brown's boy might do. He had kept
himself snugly hidden while Farmer
Brown's boy was there, and he felt
quite sure that Farmer Brown's boy
didn't know who had built the dam.
But for this very reason he might, he
just *might,* try to find out all about it,

and that would mean that Paddy would have to be always on the watch.

"But what's the use of worrying over troubles that haven't come yet, and may never come? Time enough to worry when they do come," said Paddy to himself, which shows that Paddy has a great deal of wisdom in his little brown head. "The thing for me to do now is to get ready for winter, and that means a great deal of work," he continued. "Let me see, I've got to build a house, a big, stout, warm house, where I will be warm and safe when my pond is frozen over. And I've got to lay in a supply of food, enough to last me until gentle Sister South Wind comes to pre-pare the way for lovely Mistress Spring. My, my, I can't afford to be sitting here dreaming, when there is such a lot to be done!"

With that Paddy slipped into the

water and swam all around his new pond
to make sure of just the best place to
build his house. Now placing one's
house in just the right place is a very
important matter. Some people are
dreadfully careless about this. Jimmy
Skunk, for instance, often makes the
mistake of digging his house (you know
Jimmy makes his house underground)
right where every one who happens
along that way will see it. Perhaps
that is because Jimmy is so independent
that he doesn't care who knows where he
lives.

But Paddy the Beaver never is careless. He always chooses just the very
best place. He makes sure that it is
best before he begins. So now, although
he was quite positive just where his
house should be, he swam around the
pond to make doubly sure. Then, when
he was quite satisfied, he swam over to

the place he had chosen. It was where the water was quite deep.

"There mustn't be the least chance that the ice will ever get thick enough to close up my doorway," said he, "and I'm sure it never will here. I must make the foundations strong and the walls thick. I must have plenty of mud to plaster with, and inside, up above the water, I must have the snuggest, warmest room where I can sleep in comfort. This is the place to build it, and it is high time I was at work."

With that Paddy swam over to the place where he had cut the trees for his dam, and his heart was light, for he had long ago learned that the surest way to be happy is to be busy.

X

PADDY STARTS HIS HOUSE

JERRY MUSKRAT was very much interested when he found that Paddy the Beaver, who, you know, is his cousin, was building a house. Jerry is a house-builder himself, and down deep in his heart he very much doubted if Paddy could build as good a house as he could. His house was down in the Smiling Pool, and Jerry thought it a very wonderful house indeed, and was very proud of it. It was built of mud and sod and little alder and willow twigs and bulrushes. Jerry had spent one winter in it, and he had decided to spend another there after he had fixed it up a little. So, as long as he didn't have to build a brand new house, he could afford the time to watch his cousin Paddy. Perhaps he hoped that Paddy would ask his advice.

But Paddy did nothing of the kind. He had seen Jerry Muskrat's house, and he had smiled. But he had taken great pains not to let Jerry see that smile. He wouldn't have hurt Jerry's feelings for the world. He is too polite and good-natured to do anything like that. So Jerry sat on the end of an old log and watched Paddy work. The first thing to build was the foundation. This was of mud and grass with sticks worked into it to hold it together. Paddy dug the mud from the bottom of his new pond. And because the pond was new, there was a great deal of grassy sod there, which was just what Paddy needed. It was very convenient.

Jerry watched a little while and then,

because Jerry is a worker himself, he just had to get busy and help. Rather timidly he told his big cousin that he would like to have a share in building the new house.

"All right," replied Paddy, "that will be fine. You can bring mud while I am getting the sticks and grass."

So Jerry dived down to the bottom of the pond and dug up mud and piled it on the foundation and was happy. The little stars looked down and twinkled merrily as they watched the two workers. So the foundation grew and grew down under the water. Jerry was very much surprised at the size of it. It was ever and ever so much bigger than the foundation for his own house. You see, he had forgotten how much bigger Paddy is.

Each night Jerry and Paddy worked, resting during the daytime. Occasion-

ally Bobby Coon or Reddy Fox or Unc'
Billy Possum or Jimmy Skunk would
come to the edge of the pond to see what
was going on. Peter Rabbit came every night. But they couldn't see much
because, you know, Paddy and Jerry
were working under water.

But at last Peter was rewarded.
There, just above the water, was a splendid platform of mud and grass and
sticks. A great many sticks were carefully laid as soon as the platform was
above the water, for Paddy was very
particular about this. You see, it was
to be the floor for the splendid room he
was planning to build. When it suited
him, he began to pile mud in the very
middle.

Jerry puzzled and puzzled over this.
Where was Paddy's room going to be,
if he piled up the mud that way? But
he didn't like to ask questions, so he

kept right on helping. Paddy would dive down to the bottom and then come up with double handfuls of mud, which he held against his chest. He would scramble out onto the platform and waddle over to the pile in the middle, where he would put the mud and pat it down. Then back to the bottom for more mud.

And so the mud pile grew and grew, until it was quite two feet high. "Now," said Paddy, "I'll build the walls, and I guess you can't help me much with those. I'm going to begin them to-morrow night. Perhaps you will like to see me do it, Cousin Jerry."

"I certainly will," replied Jerry, still puzzling over that pile of mud in the middle.

XI

JERRY MUSKRAT was more and
more sure that his big cousin,
Paddy the Beaver, didn't know
quite so much as he might about house-
building. Jerry would have liked to
offer some suggestions, but he didn't
quite dare. You see, he was very anx-
ious not to displease his big cousin.
But he felt that he simply had got to
speak his mind to some one, so he swam
across to where he had seen Peter Rabbit almost every night since Paddy began to build. Sure enough, Peter was
there, sitting up very straight and staring with big round eyes at the platform

"Why, it's a house, you stupid. It's Paddy's new house,"
replied Jerry. *Page 57.*

of mud and sticks out in the water where Paddy the Beaver was at work.

"Well, Peter, what do you think of it?" asked Jerry.

"What is it?" asked Peter innocently. "Is it another dam?"

Jerry threw back his head and laughed and laughed.

Peter looked at him suspiciously. "I don't see anything to laugh at," said he.

"Why, it's a house, you stupid. It's Paddy's new house," replied Jerry, wiping the tears of laughter from his eyes.

"I'm not stupid!" retorted Peter. "How was I to know that that pile of mud and sticks is meant for a house? It certainly doesn't look it. Where is the door?"

"To tell you the truth, I don't think it is much of a house myself," replied Jerry. "It has got a door, all right.

In fact, it has got three. You can't see them because they are under water, and there is a passage from each right up through that platform of mud and sticks, which is the foundation of the house. It really is a very fine foundation, Peter; it really is. But what I can't understand is what Paddy is thinking of by building that great pile of mud right in the middle. When he gets his walls built, where will his bedroom be? There won't be any room at all. It won't be a house at all —just a big useless pile of sticks and mud."

Peter scratched his head and then pulled his whiskers thoughtfully as he gazed out at the pile in the water where Paddy the Beaver was at work.

"It does look foolish, that's a fact," said he. "Why don't you point out to him the mistake he is making, Jerry?

You have built such a splendid house
yourself that you ought to be able to
help Paddy and show him his mis-
takes."

Jerry had smiled a very self-satisfied
smile when Peter mentioned his fine
house, but he shook his head at the sug-
gestion that he should give Paddy advice.

"I—I don't just like to," he confessed. "You know, he might not like
it and—and it doesn't seem as if it
would be quite polite."

Peter sniffed. "That wouldn't trouble me any if he were my cousin," said
he.

Jerry shook his head. "No, I don't
believe it would," he replied, "but it
does trouble me and—and—well, I
think I'll wait awhile."

Now all this time Paddy had been
hard at work. He was bringing the

longest branches which he had cut from
the trees out of which he had built his
dam, and a lot of slender willow and alder poles. He pushed these ahead of
him as he swam. When he reached the
foundation of his house, he would lean
them against the pile of mud in the middle with their big ends resting on the
foundation. So he worked all the way
around until by and by the mud pile in
the middle couldn't be seen. It was
completely covered with sticks, and
they were cunningly fastened together
at the tops.

XII

JERRY MUSKRAT LEARNS SOMETHING

If you think you know it all
You are riding for a fall.
Use your ears and use your eyes,
But hold your tongue and you'll be wise.

JERRY MUSKRAT will tell you that is as true as true can be. Jerry knows. He found it out for himself. Now he is very careful what he says about other people or what they are doing. But he wasn't so careful when his cousin, Paddy the Beaver, was building his house. No, Sir, Jerry wasn't so careful then. He thought he knew more about building a house than Paddy did. He was sure of it when he watched Paddy heap up a great pile of mud right in the middle where his room ought to be, and then build a wall of sticks around it. He said as much to Peter Rabbit.

Now it is never safe to say anything to Peter Rabbit that you don't care to have others know. Peter has a great deal of respect for Jerry Muskrat's opinion on house-building. You see, he very much admires Jerry's snug house in the Smiling Pool. It really is a very fine house, and Jerry may be excused for being proud of it. But that doesn't excuse Jerry for thinking that he knows all there is to know about house-building. Of course Peter told every one he met that Paddy the Beaver was making a foolish mistake in building his house, and that Jerry Muskrat, who ought to know, said so.

So whenever they got the chance, the little people of the Green Forest and the Green Meadows would steal up to the shore of Paddy's new pond and chuckle as they looked out at the great pile of sticks and mud which Paddy had built for a house, but in which he had forgotten to make a room. At least they supposed that he had forgotten this very important thing. He must have, for there wasn't any room. It was a great joke. They laughed a lot about it, and they lost a great deal of the respect for Paddy which they had had since he built his wonderful dam.

Jerry and Peter sat in the moonlight talking it over. Paddy had stopped bringing sticks for his wall. He had dived down out of sight, and he was gone a long time. Suddenly Jerry noticed that the water had grown very, very muddy all around Paddy's new house. He wrinkled his brows trying to think what Paddy could be doing.

Presently Paddy came up for air
Then he went down again, and the water grew muddier than ever. This
went on for a long time. Every little
while Paddy would come up for air and
a few minutes of rest. Then down he
would go, and the water would grow
muddier and muddier.

At last Jerry could stand it no longer.
He just had to see what was going on.
He slipped into the water and swam
over to where the water was muddiest.
Just as he got there up came Paddy.

"Hello, Cousin Jerry!" said he. "I
was just going to invite you over to see
what you think of my house inside.
Just follow me."

Paddy dived, and Jerry dived after
him. He followed Paddy in at one of
the three doorways under water and up
a smooth hall right into the biggest,
nicest bedroom Jerry had ever seen in

all his life. He just gasped in sheer surprise. He couldn't do anything else. He couldn't find his tongue to say a word. Here he was in this splendid great room up above the water, and he had been so sure that there wasn't any room at all! He just didn't know what to make of it.

Paddy's eyes twinkled. "Well," said he, "what do you think of it?"

"I—I—think it is splendid, just perfectly splendid! But I don't understand it at all, Cousin Paddy. I—I—Where is that great pile of mud I helped you build in the middle?" Jerry looked as foolish as he felt when he asked this.

"Why, I've dug it all away. That's what made the water so muddy," replied Paddy.

"But what did you build it for in the first place?" Jerry persisted.

"Because I had to have something to rest my sticks against while I was building my walls, of course," replied Paddy. "When I got the tops fastened together for a roof, they didn't need a support any longer, and then I dug it away to make this room. I couldn't have built such a big room any other way. I see you don't know very much about house-building, Cousin Jerry."

"I—I'm afraid I don't," confessed Jerry sadly.

XIII

THE QUEER STOREHOUSE

EVERYBODY knew that Paddy the Beaver was laying up a supply of food for the winter, and everybody thought it was queer food. That is, everybody but Prickly Porky the Porcupine thought so. Prickly Porky likes the same kind of food, but he never lays up a supply. He just goes out and gets it when he wants it, winter or summer. What kind of food was it? Why, bark, to be sure. Yes, Sir, it was just bark—the bark of certain kinds of trees.

Now Prickly Porky can climb the trees and eat the bark right there, but Paddy the Beaver cannot climb, and if

he should just eat the bark that he can
reach from the ground it would take
such a lot of trees to keep him filled up
that he would soon spoil the Green Forest. You know, when the bark is taken
off a tree all the way around, the tree
dies. That is because all the things
that a tree draws out of the ground to
make it grow and keep it alive are carried up from the roots in the sap, and
the sap cannot go up the tree trunks
and into the branches when the bark is
taken off, because it is up the inside of
the bark that it travels. So when the
bark is taken from a tree all the way
around the trunk, the tree just starves
to death.

Now Paddy the Beaver loves the
Green Forest as dearly as you and I do,
and perhaps even a little more dearly.
You see, it is his home. Besides,
Paddy never is wasteful. So he cuts

down a tree so that he can get all the bark instead of killing a whole lot of trees for a very little bark, as he might do if he were lazy. There isn't a lazy bone in him—not one. The bark he likes best is from the aspen. When he cannot get that, he will eat the bark from the poplar, the alder, the willow, and even the birch. But he likes the aspen so much better that he will work very hard to get it. Perhaps it tastes better because he does have to work so hard for it.

There were some aspen-trees growing right on the edge of the pond Paddy had made in the Green Forest. These he cut just as he had cut the trees for his dam. As soon as a tree was down, he would cut it into short lengths, and with these swim out to where the water was deep, close to his new house. He took them one by one and carried the first ones to the bottom, where he pushed them into the mud just enough to hold them. Then, as fast as he brought more, he piled them on the first ones. And so the pile grew and grew.

Jerry Muskrat, Peter Rabbit, Bobby Coon, and the other little people of the Green Forest watched him with the greatest interest and curiosity. They couldn't quite make out what he was doing. It was almost as if he were building the foundation for another house.

"What's he doing, Jerry?" demanded Peter, when he could keep still no longer.

"I don't exactly know," replied Jerry. "He said that he was going to lay in a supply of food for the winter, just as I told you, and I suppose that is what he is doing. But I don't quite understand what he is taking it all out into the pond for. I believe I'll go ask him."

"Do, and then come tell us," begged Peter, who was growing so curious that he couldn't sit still.

So Jerry swam out to where Paddy was so busy. "Is this your food supply, Cousin Paddy?" he asked.

"Yes," replied Paddy, crawling up on the side of his house to rest. "Yes, this is my food supply. Isn't it splendid?"

"I guess it is," replied Jerry, trying to be polite, "though I like lily-roots and clams better. But what are you going to do with it? Where is your storehouse?"

"This pond is my storehouse," replied Paddy. "I will make a great pile right here close to my house, and the water will keep it nice and fresh all winter. When the pond is frozen over, all I will have to do is to slip out of one of my doorways down there on the bottom, swim over here and get a stick, and fill my stomach.   Isn't it handy?"

XIV

A FOOTPRINT IN THE MUD

VERY early one morning Paddy the Beaver heard Sammy Jay making a terrible fuss over in the aspen-trees on the edge of the pond Paddy had made in the Green Forest. Paddy couldn't see because he was inside his house, and it has no window, but he could hear. He wrinkled up his brows thoughtfully.

"Seems to me that Sammy is very much excited this morning," said he, talking to himself, a way he has because he is so much alone. "When he screams like that, Sammy is usually trying to do two things at once—make trouble for somebody and keep somebody else out of trouble; and when you come to think of it, that's rather a funny way of doing. It shows that he isn't all bad, and at the same time he is a long way from being all good. Now, I should say from the sounds that Sammy has discovered Reddy Fox trying to steal up on some one over where my aspen-trees are growing. Reddy is afraid of me, but I suspect that he knows that Peter Rabbit has been hanging around here a lot lately, watching me work, and he thinks perhaps he can catch Peter. I shall have to whisper in one of Peter's long ears and tell him to watch out."

After a while he heard Sammy Jay's voice growing fainter and fainter in the Green Forest. Finally he couldn't hear it at all. "Whoever was there has gone away, and Sammy has followed just to torment them," thought Paddy.

He was very busy making a bed. He is very particular about his bed, is Paddy the Beaver. He makes it of fine splinters of wood which he splits off with those wonderful great cutting teeth of his. This makes the driest kind of a bed. It requires a great deal of patience and work, but patience is one of the first things a little Beaver learns, and honest work well done is one of the greatest pleasures in the world, as Paddy long ago found out for himself. So he kept at work on his bed for some time after all was still outside.

At last Paddy decided that he would go over to his aspen-trees and look them over to decide which ones he would cut the next night. He slid down one of his long halls, out the doorway at the bottom of the pond, and then swam up to the surface, where he floated for a few minutes with just his head out of water. And all the time his eyes and nose and ears were busy looking, smelling, and listening for any sign of danger. Everything was still. Sure that he was quite safe, Paddy swam across to the place where the aspen-trees grew, and waddled out on the shore.

Paddy looked this way and looked that way. He looked up in the tree tops, and he looked off up the hill, but most of all he looked at the ground. Yes, Sir, Paddy just studied the ground. You see, he hadn't forgotten the fuss Sammy Jay had been making there, and he was trying to find out what it was all about. At first he didn't see anything unusual, but by and by he happened to notice a little wet place, and right in the middle of it was something that made Paddy's eyes open wide. It was a footprint! Some one had carelessly stepped in the mud.

"Ha!" exclaimed Paddy, and the hair on his back lifted ever so little, and for a minute he had a prickly feeling all over. The footprint was very much like that of Reddy Fox, only it was larger.

"Ha!" said Paddy again, "that certainly is the footprint of Old Man Coyote! I see I have got to watch out, more sharply than I had thought for. All right, Mr. Coyote; now that I know you are about, you'll have to be smarter than I think you are to catch me. You certainly will be back here to-night looking for me, so I think I'll do my cutting right now in the daytime."

XV

SAMMY JAY MAKES PADDY A CALL

PADDY THE BEAVER was hard at work. He had just cut down a good-sized aspen-tree and now he was gnawing it into short lengths to put in his food pile in the pond. As he worked, Paddy was doing a lot of thinking about the footprint of Old Man Coyote in a little patch of mud, for he knew that meant that Old Man Coyote had discovered his pond, and would be hanging around, hoping to catch Paddy off his guard. Paddy knew it just as well as if Old Man Coyote had told him so. That was why he was at work cutting his food supply in the daytime. Usually he works at night, and he knew that Old Man Coyote knew it.

"He'll try to catch me then," thought Paddy, "so I'll do my working on land now and fool him."

The tree he was cutting began to sway and crack. Paddy cut out one more big chip, then hurried away to a safe place while the tree fell with a crash.

"Thief! thief! thief!" screamed a voice just back of Paddy.

"Hello, Sammy Jay! I see you don't feel any better than usual this morning," said Paddy. "Don't you want to sit up in this tree while I cut it down?"

Sammy grew black in the face with anger, for he knew that Paddy was laughing at him. You remember how only a few days before he had been so intent on calling Paddy bad names that

he actually hadn't noticed that Paddy
was cutting the very tree in which he
was sitting, and so when it fell he had
had a terrible fright.

"You think you are very smart, Mr.
Beaver, but you'll think differently one
of these fine days!" screamed Sammy.
"If you knew what I know, you
wouldn't be so well satisfied with yourself."

"What do you know?" asked Paddy,
pretending to be very much alarmed.

"I'm not going to tell you what I
know," retorted Sammy Jay. "You'll
find out soon enough. And when you
do find out, you'll never steal another
tree from our Green Forest. Somebody is going to catch you, and it isn't
Farmer Brown's boy either!"

Paddy pretended to be terribly
frightened. "Oh, who is it? Please
tell me, Mr. Jay," he begged.

Now to be called Mr. Jay made Sammy feel very important. Nearly everybody else called him Sammy. He swelled himself out trying to look as important as he felt, and his eyes snapped with pleasure. He was actually making Paddy the Beaver afraid. At least he thought he was.

"No, Sir, I won't tell you," he replied. "I wouldn't be you for a great deal though! Somebody who is smarter than you are is going to catch you, and when he gets through with you, there won't be anything left but a few bones. No, Sir, nothing but a few bones!"

"Oh, Mr. Jay, this is terrible news! Whatever am I to do?" cried Paddy, all the time keeping right on at work cutting another tree.

"There's nothing you can do," replied Sammy, grinning wickedly at

Paddy's fright. "There's nothing you can do unless you go right straight back to the North where you came from. You think you are very smart but—"

Sammy didn't finish. Crack! Over fell the tree Paddy had been cutting and the top of it fell straight into the alder in which Sammy was sitting. "Oh! Oh! Help!" shrieked Sammy, spreading his wings and flying away just in time.

Paddy sat down and laughed until his sides ached. "Come make me another call some day, Sammy!" he said. "And when you do, please bring some real news. I know all about Old Man Coyote. You can tell him for me that when he is planning to catch people he should be careful not to leave footprints to give himself away."

Sammy didn't reply. He just sneaked off through the Green Forest, looking quite as foolish as he felt.

XVI

OLD MAN COYOTE IS VERY CRAFTY

Coyote has a crafty brain;
His wits are sharp his ends to gain.

THERE is nothing in the world more true than that. Old Man Coyote has the craftiest brain of all the little people of the Green Forest or the Green Meadows. Sharp as are the wits of old Granny Fox, they are not quite as sharp as the wits of Old Man Coyote. If you want to fool him, you will have to get up very early in the morning, and then it is more than likely that you will be the one fooled, not he. There is very little going on around him that he doesn't know about. But once in a while something escapes him. The coming of Paddy the Beaver to the

Green Forest was one of these things.
He didn't know a thing about Paddy
until Paddy had finished his dam and
his house, and was cutting his supply
of food for the winter.

You see, it was this way: When the
Merry Little Breezes of Old Mother
West Wind first heard what was going
on in the Green Forest and hurried
around over the Green Meadows and
through the Green Forest to spread the
news, as is their way, they took the
greatest pains not to even hint it to Old
Man Coyote because they were afraid
that he would make trouble and perhaps drive Paddy away. The place
that Paddy had chosen to build his dam
was so deep in the Green Forest that
Old Man Coyote seldom went that way.
So it was that he knew nothing about
Paddy, and Paddy knew nothing about
him for some time.

But after a while Old Man Coyote
noticed that the little people of the
Green Meadows were not about as much
as usual. They seemed to have a se-
cret of some kind. He mentioned the
matter to his friend, Digger the
Badger.

Digger had been so intent on his own
affairs that he hadn't noticed anything
unusual, but when Old Man Coyote
mentioned the matter he remembered
that Blacky the Crow headed straight
for the Green Forest every morning.
Several times he had seen Sammy Jay
flying in the same direction as if in a
great hurry to get somewhere.

Old Man Coyote grinned. "That's
all I need to know, friend Digger," said
he. "When Blacky the Crow and
Sammy Jay visit a place more than
once, something interesting is going on
there. I think I'll take a stroll up

through the Green Forest and have a look around."

With that, off Old Man Coyote started. But he was too sly and crafty to go straight to the Green Forest. He pretended to hunt around over the Green Meadows just as he usually did, all the time working nearer and nearer to the Green Forest. When he reached the edge of it, he slipped in among the trees, and when he felt sure that no one was likely to see him, he began to run this way and that way with his nose to the ground.

"Ha!" he exclaimed presently, "Reddy Fox has been this way lately."

Pretty soon he found another trail. "So," said he, "Peter Rabbit has been over here a good deal of late, and his trail goes in the same direction as that of Reddy Fox. I guess all I have to do now is to follow Peter's trail, and it will lead me to what I want to find out."

So Old Man Coyote followed Peter's trail, and he presently came to the pond of Paddy the Beaver. "Ha!" said he, as he looked out and saw Paddy's new house. "So there is a newcomer to the Green Forest! I have always heard that Beaver is very good eating. My stomach begins to feel empty this very minute." His mouth began to water, and a fierce, hungry look shone in his yellow eyes.

It was just then that Sammy Jay saw him and began to scream at the top of his lungs so that Paddy the Beaver over in his house heard him. Old Man Coyote knew that it was of no use to stay longer with Sammy Jay about, so he took a hasty look at the pond and found where Paddy came ashore to cut his food. Then, shaking his fist at

Sammy Jay, he started straight back for the Green Meadows. "I'll just pay a visit here in the night," said he, "and give Mr. Beaver a surprise while he is at work."

But with all his craft, Old Man Coyote didn't notice that he had left a footprint in the mud.

XVII

OLD MAN COYOTE lay stretched out in his favorite napping place on the Green Meadows. He was thinking of what he had found out up in the Green Forest that morning--that Paddy the Beaver was living there. Old Man Coyote's thoughts seemed very pleasant to himself, though really they were very dreadful thoughts. You see, he was thinking how easy it was going to be to catch Paddy the Beaver, and what a splendid meal he would make. He licked his chops at the thought.

"He doesn't know I know he's here," thought Old Man Coyote. "In fact, I don't believe he even knows that I am anywhere around. Of course, he won't be watching for me. He cuts his trees at night, so all I will have to do is to hide right close by where he is at work, and he'll walk right into my mouth. Sammy Jay knows I was up there this morning, but Sammy sleeps at night, so he will not give the alarm. My, my, how good that Beaver will taste!" He licked his chops once more, then yawned and closed his eyes for a nap.

Old Man Coyote waited until jolly, round, red Mr. Sun had gone to bed behind the Purple Hills, and the Black Shadows had crept out across the Green Meadows. Then, keeping in the blackest of them, and looking very much like a shadow himself, he slipped into the Green Forest. It was dark in there, and he made straight for Paddy's new pond, trotting along swiftly without making a sound. When he was near the aspen-trees which he knew Paddy was planning to cut, he crept forward very slowly and carefully. Everything was still as still could be.

"Good!" thought Old Man Coyote. "I am here first, and now all I need do is to hide and wait for Paddy to come ashore."

So he stretched himself flat behind some brush close beside the little path Paddy had made up from the edge of the water and waited. It was very still, so still that it seemed almost as if he could hear his heart beat. He could see the little stars twinkling in the sky and their own reflections twinkling back at them from the water of Paddy's pond. Old Man Coyote waited and waited. He is very patient when there is something to gain by it. For such a splendid dinner as Paddy the Beaver

would make he felt that he could well
afford to be patient. So he waited and
waited, and everything was as still as
if no living thing but the trees were
there. Even the trees seemed to be
asleep.

At last, after a long, long time, he
heard just the faintest splash. He
pricked up his ears and peeped out on
the pond with the hungriest look in his
yellow eyes. There was a little line of
silver coming straight towards him.
He knew that it was made by Paddy
the Beaver swimming. Nearer and
nearer it drew. Old Man Coyote
chuckled way down deep inside, without making a sound. He could see
Paddy's head now, and Paddy was
coming straight in, as if he hadn't a
fear in the world.

Almost to the edge of the pond swam
Paddy. Then he stopped. In a few

minutes he began to swim again, but this time it was back in the direction of his house, and he seemed to be carrying something. It was one of the little food logs he had cut that day, and he was taking it out to his storehouse. Then back he came for another. And so he kept on, never once coming ashore. Old Man Coyote waited until Paddy had carried the last log to his storehouse and then, with a loud whack on the water with his broad tail, had dived and disappeared in his house.

Then Old Man Coyote arose and started elsewhere to look for his dinner, and in his heart was bitter disappointment.

XVIII

OLD MAN COYOTE TRIES ANOTHER PLAN.

FOR three nights Old Man Coyote had stolen up through the Green Forest with the coming of the Black Shadows and had hidden among the aspen-trees where Paddy the Beaver cut his food, and for three nights Paddy had failed to come ashore. Each night he had seemed to have enough food logs in the water to keep him busy without cutting more. Old Man Coyote lay there, and the hungry look in his eyes changed to one of doubt and then to suspicion. Could it be that Paddy the Beaver was smarter than he thought? It began to look very much as if Paddy knew perfectly well that he was hiding there each night. Yes, Sir, that's the way it looked. For three nights Paddy hadn't cut a single tree, and yet each night he had plenty of food logs ready to take to his storehouse in the pond.

"That means that he comes ashore in the daytime and cuts his trees," thought Old Man Coyote as, tired and with black anger in his heart, he trotted home the third night. "He couldn't have found out about me himself; he isn't smart enough. It must be that some one has told him. And nobody knows that I have been over there but Sammy Jay. It must be he who has been the tattletale. I think I'll visit Paddy by daylight to-morrow, and then we'll see!"

Now the trouble with some smart people is that they are never able to believe that others may be as smart as they. Old Man Coyote didn't know that the first time he had visited Paddy's pond he had left behind him a footprint in a little patch of soft mud. If he had known it, he wouldn't have believed that Paddy would be smart enough to guess what that footprint meant. So Old Man Coyote laid all the blame at the door of Sammy Jay, and that very morning, when Sammy came flying over the Green Meadows, Old Man Coyote accused him of being a tattletale and threatened the most dreadful things to Sammy if ever he caught him.

Now Sammy had flown down to the Green Meadows to tell Old Man Coyote how Paddy was doing all his work on land in the daytime. But when Old Man Coyote began to call him a tattletale and accuse him of having warned Paddy, and to threaten dreadful things, he straightway forgot all his anger at

Paddy and turned it all on Old Man Coyote. He called him everything he could think of, and this was a great deal, for Sammy has a wicked tongue. When he hadn't any breath left, he flew over to the Green Forest, and there he hid where he could watch all that was going on.

That afternoon Old Man Coyote tried his new plan. He slipped into the Green Forest, looking this way and that way to be sure that no one saw him. Then very, very softly, he crept up through the Green Forest towards the pond of Paddy the Beaver. As he drew near, he heard a crash, and it made him smile. He knew what it meant. It meant that Paddy was at work cutting down trees. With his stomach almost on the ground, he crept forward little by little, little by little, taking the greatest care not to rustle so much as a leaf. Presently he reached a place where he could see the aspen trees, and there sure enough was Paddy, sitting up on his hind legs and hard at work cutting another tree.

Old Man Coyote lay down for a few minutes to watch. Then he wriggled a little nearer. Slowly and carefully he drew his legs under him and made ready for a rush. Paddy the Beaver was his at last! At just that very minute a harsh scream rang out right over his head "Thief! thief! thief!"

It was Sammy Jay, who had silently followed him all the way. Paddy the Beaver didn't stop to even look around. He knew what that scream meant, and he scrambled down his little path to the water as he never had scrambled before. And as he dived with a great splash, Old Man Coyote landed with a great jump on the very edge of the pond.

XIX

PADDY THE BEAVER floated in his pond and grinned in the most provoking way at Old Man Coyote, who had so nearly caught him. Old Man Coyote fairly danced with anger on the bank. He had felt so sure of Paddy that time that it was hard work to believe that Paddy had really gotten away from him. He bared his long cruel teeth, and he looked very fierce and ugly.

"Come on in; the water's fine!" called Paddy.

Now, of course, this wasn't a nice thing for Paddy to do, for it only made Old Man Coyote all the angrier. You see, Paddy knew perfectly well that he was absolutely safe, and he just couldn't resist the temptation to say some unkind things. He had had to be on the watch for days lest he should be caught, and so he hadn't been able to work quite so well as he could have done with nothing to fear, and he still had a lot of preparations to make for winter. So he told Old Man Coyote just what he thought of him, and that he wasn't as smart as he thought he was or he never would have left a footprint in the mud to give him away.

When Sammy Jay, who was listening and chuckling as he listened, heard that, he flew down where he would be just out of reach of Old Man Coyote, and then he just turned that tongue of his loose, and you know that some people say that Sammy's tongue is hung in the middle and wags at both ends. Of course, this isn't really so, but when he gets to abusing people it seems as if it must be true. He called Old Man Coyote every bad name he could think of. He called him a sneak, a thief, a coward, a bully, and a lot of other things.

"You said I had warned Paddy that you were trying to catch him and that was why you failed to find him at work at night, and all the time you had warned him yourself!" screamed Sammy. "I used to think that you were smart, but I know better now. Paddy is twice as smart as you are."

> Mr. Coyote is ever so sly;
> Mr. Coyote is clever and spry;
>   If you believe all you hear.
> Mr. Coyote is naught of the kind;
> Mr. Coyote is stupid and blind;
>   He can't catch a flea on his ear."

Paddy the Beaver laughed till the tears came at Sammy's foolish verse,

but it made Old Man Coyote angrier
than ever. He was angry with Paddy
for escaping from him, and he was angry with Sammy, terribly angry, and
the worst of it was he couldn't catch
either one, for one was at home in the
water and the other was at home in the
air and he couldn't follow in either
place. Finally he saw it was of no use
to stay there to be laughed at, so, mut-
tering and grumbling, he started for
the Green Meadows.

As soon as he was out of sight Paddy
turned to Sammy Jay.

"Mr. Jay," said he, knowing how it
pleased Sammy to be called mister,
"Mr. Jay, you have done me a mighty
good turn to-day, and I am not going
to forget it. You can call me what you
please and scream at me all you please,
but you won't get any satisfaction out
of it, because I simply won't get angry.

I will say to myself, 'Mr. Jay saved my life the other day,' and then I won't mind your tongue."

Now this made Sammy feel very proud and very happy. You know it is very seldom that he hears anything nice said of him. He flew down on the stump of one of the trees Paddy had cut. "Let's be friends," said he.

"With all my heart!" replied Paddy.

XX

SAMMY JAY OFFERS TO HELP PADDY

PADDY sat looking thoughtfully at the aspen-trees he would have to cut to complete his store of food for the winter. All those near the edge of his pond had been cut. The others were scattered about some little distance away. "I don't know," said Paddy out loud. "I don't know."

"What don't you know?" asked Sammy Jay, who, now that he and Paddy had become friends, was very much interested in what Paddy was doing.

"Why," replied Paddy, "I don't know just how I am going to get those trees. Now that Old Man Coyote is watching for me, it isn't safe for me to

go very far from my pond. I suppose
I could dig a canal up to some of the
nearest trees and then float them down
to the pond, but it is hard to work and
keep sharp watch for enemies at the
same time. I guess I'll have to be con-
tent with some of these alders growing
close to the water, but the bark of as-
pens is so much better that I—I wish
I could get them."

"What's a canal?" asked Sammy ab-
ruptly.

"A canal? Why, a canal is a kind
of ditch in which water can run," replied Paddy.

Sammy nodded. "I've seen Farmer
Brown dig one over on the Green
Meadows, but it looked like a great deal
of work. I didn't suppose that any one
else could do it. Do you really mean
that you can dig a canal, Paddy?"

"Of course I mean it," replied Paddy,

in a surprised tone of voice. "I have
helped dig lots of canals. You ought
to see some of them back where I came
from."

"I'd like to," replied Sammy. "I
think it is perfectly wonderful. I
don't see how you do it."

"It's easy enough when you know
how," replied Paddy. "If I dared to,
I'd show you."

Sammy had a sudden idea. It almost made him gasp. "I tell you what,
you work and I'll keep watch!" he
cried. "You know my eyes are very
sharp."

"Will you?" cried Paddy eagerly.
"That would be perfectly splendid.
You have the sharpest eyes of any one
whom I know, and I would feel perfectly safe with you on watch. But I
don't want to put you to all that trouble,
Mr. Jay."

"Of course I will," replied Sammy, "and it won't be any trouble at all. I'll just love to do it." You see, it made Sammy feel very proud to have Paddy say that he had such sharp eyes. "When will you begin?"

"Right away, if you will just take a look around and see that it is perfectly safe for me to come out on land."

Sammy didn't wait to hear more. He spread his beautiful blue wings and started off over the Green Forest straight for the Green Meadows. Paddy watched him go with a puzzled and disappointed air. "That's funny," thought he. "I thought he really meant it, and now off he goes without even saying good-by."

In a little while back came Sammy, all out of breath. "It's all right," he panted. "You can go to work just as soon as you please."

Paddy looked more puzzled than ever. "How do you know?" he asked. "I haven't seen you looking around."

"I did better than that," replied Sammy. "If Old Man Coyote had been hiding somewhere in the Green Forest, it might have taken me some time to find him. But he isn't. You see, I flew straight over to his home in the Green Meadows to see if he is there, and he is. He's taking a sun-bath and looking as cross as two sticks. I don't think he'll be back here this morning, but I'll keep a sharp watch while you work."

Paddy made Sammy a low bow. "You certainly are smart, Mr. Jay," said he. "I wouldn't have thought of going over to Old Man Coyote's home to see if he was there. I'll feel perfectly safe with you on guard. Now I'll get to work."

XXI

PADDY AND SAMMY JAY WORK TOGETHER

JERRY MUSKRAT had been home at the Smiling Pool for several days. But he couldn't stay there long. Oh, my, no! He just had to get back to see what his big cousin, Paddy the Beaver, was doing. So as soon as he was sure that everything was all right at the Smiling Pool he hurried back up the Laughing Brook to Paddy's pond, deep in the Green Forest. As soon as he was in sight of it, he looked eagerly for Paddy. At first he didn't see him. Then he stopped and gazed over at the place where Paddy had been cutting aspen-trees for food. Something was going on there, something queer. He couldn't make it out.

Just then Sammy Jay came flying over.

"What's Paddy doing?" Jerry asked.

Sammy Jay dropped down to the top of an alder-tree and fluffed out all his feathers in a very important way. "Oh," said he, "Paddy and I are building something!"

"You! Paddy and you! Ha, ha! Paddy and you building something!" Jerry laughed.

"Yes, me!" snapped Sammy angrily. "That's what I said; Paddy and I are building something."

Jerry had begun to swim across the pond by this time, and Sammy was flying across. "Why don't you tell the truth, Sammy, and say that Paddy is building something and you are making him all the trouble you can?" called Jerry.

Sammy's eyes snapped angrily, and he darted down at Jerry's little brown head. "It isn't true!" he shrieked. "You ask Paddy if I'm not helping!"

Jerry ducked under water to escape Sammy's sharp bill. When he came up again, Sammy was over in the little grove of aspen-trees where Paddy was at work. Then Jerry discovered something. What was it? Why a little water-path led right up to the aspen-trees, and there, at the end of the little water-path, was Paddy the Beaver hard at work. He was digging and piling the earth on one side very neatly. In fact, he was making the water-path longer. Jerry swam right up the little water-path to where Paddy was working. "Good morning, Cousin Paddy," said he. "What are you doing?"

"Oh," replied Paddy, "Sammy Jay and I are building a canal."

Sammy Jay looked down at Jerry in triumph, and Jerry looked at Paddy as if he thought that he was joking.

"Sammy Jay? What's Sammy Jay got to do about it?" demanded Jerry.

"A whole lot," replied Paddy. "You see, he keeps watch while I work. If he didn't, I couldn't work, and there wouldn't be any canal. Old Man Coyote has been trying to catch me, and I wouldn't dare work on shore if it wasn't that I am sure that the sharpest eyes in the Green Forest are watching for danger."

Sammy Jay looked very much pleased indeed and very proud. "So you see it takes both of us to make this canal; I dig while Sammy watches. So we are building it together," concluded Paddy with a twinkle in his eyes.

"I see," said Jerry slowly. Then he turned to Sammy Jay. "I beg your

pardon, Sammy," said he. "I do, indeed."

"That's all right," replied Sammy
airily. "What do you think of our
canal?"

"I think it is wonderful," replied
Jerry.

And indeed it was a very fine canal,
straight, wide, and deep enough for
Paddy to swim in and float his logs out
to the pond. Yes, indeed, it was a very
fine canal.

XXII

PADDY FINISHES HIS HARVEST

"Sharp his tongue and sharp his eyes—
Sammy guards against surprise.
If 'twere not for Sammy Jay
I could do no work to-day."

WHEN Sammy overheard Paddy the Beaver say that to Jerry Muskrat, it made him swell up all over with pure pride. You see, Sammy is so used to hearing bad things about himself that to hear something nice like that pleased him immensely. He straightway forgot all the mean things he had said to Paddy when he first saw him—how he had called him a thief because he had cut the aspen-trees he needed. He forgot all this.

He forgot how Paddy had made him the laughing-stock of the Green Forest and the Green Meadows by cutting down the very tree in which he had been sitting. He forgot everything but that Paddy had trusted him to keep watch and now was saying nice things about him. He made up his mind that he would deserve all the nice things that Paddy could say, and he thought that Paddy was the finest fellow in the world.

Jerry Muskrat looked doubtful. He didn't trust Sammy, and he took care not to go far from the water when he heard that Old Man Coyote had been hanging around. But Paddy worked away just as if he hadn't a fear in the world.

"The way to make people want to be trusted is to trust them," said he to himself. "If I show Sammy Jay that

I don't really trust him, he will think
it is of no use to try and will give it up.
But if I do trust him, and he knows
that I do, he'll be the best watchman
in the Green Forest."

And this shows that Paddy the
Beaver has a great deal of wisdom, for
it was just as he thought. Sammy was
on hand bright and early every morning. He made sure that Old Man
Coyote was nowhere in the Green Forest, and then he settled himself com-
fortably in the top of a tall pine-tree
where he could see all that was going on while Paddy the Beaver
worked.

Paddy had finished his canal, and a
beautiful canal it was, leading straight
from his pond up to the aspen-trees.
As soon as he had finished it, he began
to cut the trees. As soon as one was
down he would cut it into short lengths

and roll them into the canal. Then he would float them out to his pond and over to his storehouse. He took the larger branches, on which there was sweet, tender bark, in the same way, for Paddy is never wasteful.

After a while he went over to his storehouse, which, you know, was nothing but a great pile of aspen-logs and branches in his pond close by his house. He studied it very carefully. Then he swam back and climbed up on the bank of his canal.

"Mr. Jay," said he, "I think our work is about finished."

"What!" cried Sammy, "Aren't you going to cut the rest of those aspen-trees?"

"No," replied Paddy. "Enough is always enough, and I've got enough to last me all winter. I want those trees for next year. Now I am fixed for the winter. I think I'll take it easy for a while."

Sammy looked disappointed. You see he had just begun to learn that the greatest pleasure in the world comes from doing things for other people. For the first time since he could remember some one wanted him around and it gave him such a good feeling down deep inside!

THE END